This Book Belongs To
Lynn Palmer

FOR JAMES

P.A.

This is a Borzoi Book published by Alfred A. Knopf, Inc.
Text copyright © 1988 by Pam Ayres
Illustrations copyright © 1988 by Graham Percy
All rights reserved under International and Pan-American Copyright Conventions.
Published in the United States by Alfred A. Knopf, Inc., New York.
Distributed by Random House, Inc., New York.
Originally published in Great Britain
by Walker Books, Ltd., London.

First American Edition 1988.

Printed in Italy   1   2   3   4   5   6   7   8   9   0

Library of Congress Cataloging-in-Publication Data
Ayres, Pam. 1947—   .
When Dad cuts down the chestnut tree.
Summary: The prospect of seeing the chestnut
tree cut down makes a child think of all the good
things that will come from its removal; but then
come thoughts about all the good reasons for
letting the tree stay where it is.
[1. Trees—Fiction.   2. Stories in rhyme]
I. Percy, Graham. ill.   II. Title.
PZ7.A96Wg   1988   [E]   87-35299
ISBN 0-394-80435-X   ISBN 0-394-90435-4 (lib. bdg.)

WHEN DAD CUTS DOWN THE CHESTNUT TREE

by PAM AYRES

Illustrated by GRAHAM PERCY

ALFRED A. KNOPF · NEW YORK

When Dad cuts down the chestnut tree,

He'll make such things for you and me...

A rocking horse to ride all day,

A fort where all my soldiers stay.

A little barrow painted blue,

A faithful duck on wheels for you.

Stilts to make us very tall,

Colored bricks to build a wall.

When the tree is on the ground,
All my friends will come around.

The trunk will be such fun to climb.
We will have the greatest time!

No more tearing jacket sleeves,

No more trouble clearing leaves.

And when I'm tucked into my bed,
Kisses kissed and goodnights said,

The tree won't scare me anymore,
When the night wind makes it roar.

But if there wasn't any tree
What difference would it make to me?

No treehouse—that's the worst of all—
To hide in when we hear Mom call.

No cool places in the shade,
After all our games are played.

No piles of leaves to dive into—
That's something we both love to do!

No sticks to find on chilly days,
To make our winter fires blaze.

And there's still another thing—
What will happen to our swing?

Where will owl and squirrel stay
If the tree is hauled away?

If the tree is really gone,
What can I hang my birdhouse on?

Now we know our chestnut tree
Means lots of things to you and me.

Trees are special, large or small,
So Dad—don't cut it down *at all*!